GROSSET & DUNLAP
Penguin Young Readers Group
An Imprint of Penguin Random House LLC

The publisher does not have any control over and does not assume any responsibility for author or third-party websites or their content.

To find out more about Eric Carle and his books, please visit eric-carle.com
To learn about The Eric Carle Museum of Picture Book Art, please visit carlemuseum.org

ISBN 9780451533463

10 9 8 7 6 5 4

I ♥ MOM

with The Very Hungry Caterpillar

Eric Carle

Grosset & Dunlap
An Imprint of Penguin Random House

Mom...

You **lift** me up,

and **hold** me close.

You are so wise,

and you **never** forget me.

Even when . . .

I **monKey** around,

or get **snappy.**

you show
me the way,

and help me

find my feet.

That's **why**...

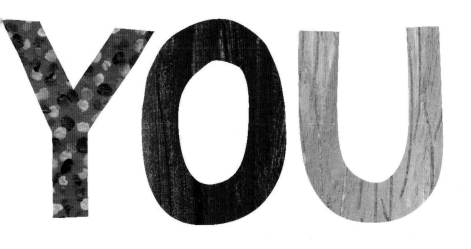